MARVEL
SPIDER-MAN

pi kids ®

An imprint of Phoenix International Publications, Inc.

Chicago • London • New York • Hamburg • Mexico City • Sydney

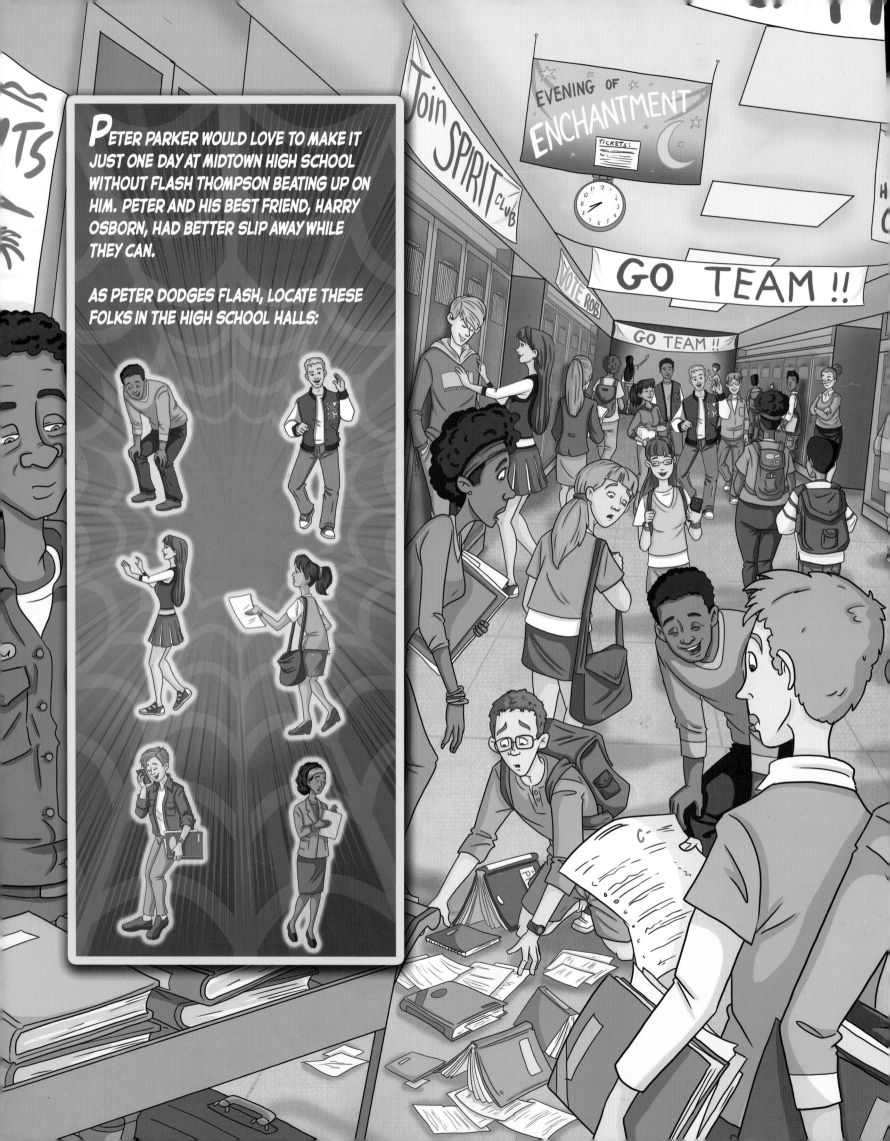

THE CITY IS RIFE WITH CRIMINALS! J. JONAH JAMESON WANTS PETER TO HIT THE STREETS AND SNAP AS MANY FRONT-PAGE PHOTOS FOR THE *DAILY BUGLE* AS HE CAN.

AS PETER COLLECTS HIS ASSIGNMENTS, SPOT THESE HOT HEADLINES:

DAILY BUGLE
Brooklyn Bridge Site of BATTLE!

DAILY BUGLE
SPIDER-MAN Captures Lizard

DAILY BUGLE
Green Goblin Robs National Bank!

DAILY BUGLE
SPIDER-MAN a MENACE?

DAILY BUGLE
WHO IS SPIDER-MAN?

DAILY BUGLE
JAMESON Wins Award!

DAILY BUGLE
Massive Power Outage Blamed on Electro

JAMESON Editor

WHAT BETTER WAY TO OBTAIN PHOTOS FOR THE *DAILY BUGLE* THAN BY FIGHTING THE CRIME FRONT AND CENTER? DOC OCK IS ATTEMPTING TO ROB AN ART MUSEUM, BUT SPIDER-MAN INTENDS TO LEAVE A LASTING IMPRESSION.

AS DOC OCK PURLOINS OLD PAINTINGS, FIND THESE OTHER INVALUABLE ARTIFACTS:

THIS SCULPTURE

THIS PAINTING

THIS PAINTING

THIS PAINTING

THIS PAINTING

THIS SCULPTURE

THIS PAINTING

VENOM IS CAUSING A GRIDLOCK! SPIDER-MAN SWINGS OVER TO INVESTIGATE, BUT HE SOON REALIZES KRAVEN HAS LURED HIM INTO A TRAP.

AS KRAVEN HUNTS BOTH HIS ELUSIVE ADVERSARIES, LOOK FOR THESE TYPES OF TRANSPORTATION:

THIS AIRPLANE

THIS AIRPLANE

THIS SAILBOAT

THIS VAN

THIS HELICOPTER

THIS VAN

THIS MOTORIST

THIS BOAT

BENEATH THE CITY'S SURFACE, LIZARD UNLEASHES HIS ATTACK. CAN SPIDEY SUBDUE THE RAMBUNCTIOUS REPTILE BEFORE THE SEWERS FLOOD?

WHILE LIZARD TRIES TO FLUSH SPIDER-MAN FROM THE SEWER SYSTEM, LOOK FOR THESE DISCARDED OBJECTS:

NEWSPAPER

MIRROR

STUFFED BEAR

BOOT

GLASSES

CAN

MYSTERIO, A MASTER OF ILLUSION, HAS SPIDER-MAN SEEING DOUBLE...AND TRIPLE! SPIDEY WILL HAVE TO GET TO THE REAL MYSTERIO IF HE WANTS TO BREAK THE SPELL.

WHILE SPIDER-MAN BATTLES HIS WAY PAST HIMSELF, SINGLE OUT THESE PETER PARKER IMPOSTORS:

MAGIC!!!

After this spectacular sensation of a day, Peter Parker has more than enough photos for the *Daily Bugle*. But Electro has just emerged, and he's trying to absorb the electricity from the subway system!

Spot these transit-takers as Spidey evades Electro's vicious voltage:

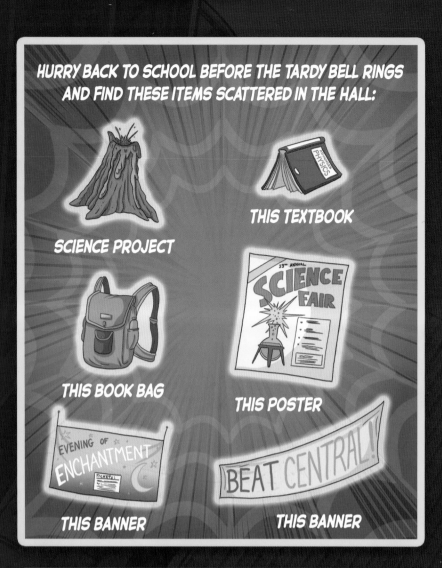

HURRY BACK TO SCHOOL BEFORE THE TARDY BELL RINGS AND FIND THESE ITEMS SCATTERED IN THE HALL:

SCIENCE PROJECT

THIS TEXTBOOK

THIS BOOK BAG

THIS POSTER

THIS BANNER

THIS BANNER

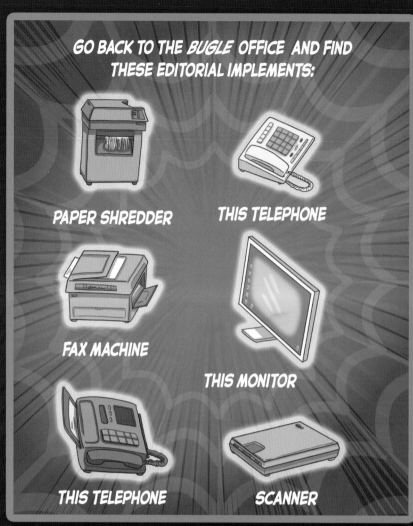

GO BACK TO THE *BUGLE* OFFICE AND FIND THESE EDITORIAL IMPLEMENTS:

PAPER SHREDDER

THIS TELEPHONE

FAX MACHINE

THIS MONITOR

THIS TELEPHONE

SCANNER

TAKE ANOTHER TOUR THROUGH THE ART MUSEUM AND POINT OUT THESE VILLAINOUS VISAGES:

MYSTERIO

ELECTRO

LIZARD

DOC OCK

SANDMAN

KRAVEN

GREEN GOBLIN

BUSTLE BACK TO THE BRIDGE AND FIND 8 OF KRAVEN'S HUNTING SPEARS.

TRUDGE BACK THROUGH THE SEWER SLUDGE TO FIND THESE INDUSTRIAL ITEMS:

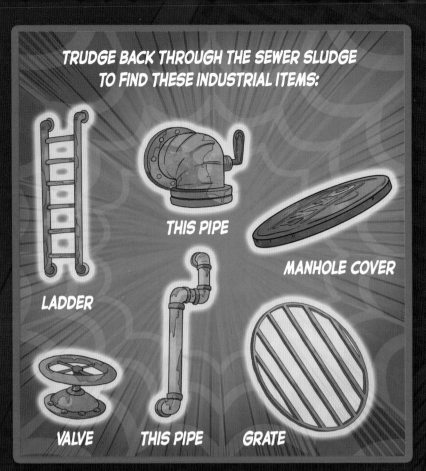

LADDER

THIS PIPE

MANHOLE COVER

VALVE

THIS PIPE

GRATE

PASS THE TIME IN LINE AT THE AMUSEMENT PARK BY FINDING 20 TUFTS OF COTTON CANDY.

REVISIT MYSTERIO'S MIND-BENDING ILLUSION AND SPOT THESE ALLURING ADVERTISEMENTS:

CAUTION: ELECTRO'S HIGH VOLTAGE IS HAZARDOUS TO YOUR HEALTH! SCURRY BACK TO THE SUBWAY TO SPOT—AND STEER CLEAR OF—THESE ERRATIC BOLTS OF ELECTRICITY:

IN A HURRY TO VANQUISH VILLAINS AROUND EVERY CORNER, SPIDER-MAN MANAGED TO DROP SOME OF HIS BEST SNAPSHOTS FOR THE *DAILY BUGLE.* GO BACK AND FIND ONE DROPPED PHOTOGRAPH IN EACH LOCATION— J. JONAH JAMESON WON'T TAKE NO FOR AN ANSWER.